First published in the United States and Canada in 2013 by Lemniscaat USA LLC •
New York
Distributed in the United States by Lemniscaat USA LLC • New York

Library of Congress Cataloging-in-Publication Data is available.
ISBN 13: 978-1-935954-27-9 (Hardcover)
Printing and binding: Worzalla, Stevens Point, WI USA
First U.S. edition

How Much Does the Gray in an Elephant Weigh?

Elle van Lieshout & Erik van Os
Illustrations Alice Hoogstad
Adapted by MaryChris Bradley

Lemniscaat

When you visit at the zoo,
Do you wonder like I do . . .

Why does giraffe have spots of brown,
And do zebra's stripes go *up, or down?*

And would the peacock ever fail,
An eye test that includes his tail?

And have you noticed as he grows,
That the snake looks like a hose?

And do you think the rhino sees,
His horn is where his nose should be?

And when they're faced
with summer's heat,
Do polar bears eat frozen treats?

And how did the elephant
come to weigh,
So very many pounds of gray?

And do flamingo's necks get tangled,
When they dance the wild fandango?

And would it not take quite a while,
To count the teeth of a crocodile?

And if a trip was their desire,
Would kangaroos a bag require?

And how would someone ever tame,
The lion's wild and wooly mane?

Our visit's done, we are on our way,
And Grandpa has one more thing to say.
"My dear child, do you ever wonder why
You don't have two noses and just one eye?"